OLIVER

A Story About Adoption

OLIVER
A Story About Adoption

Written by Lois Wickstrom

Illustrated by Priscilla Marden

OUR CHILD PRESS
800 MAPLE GLEN LANE
WAYNE PA 19087-4797

ISBN: 09611872-5-5
Previously ISBN: 0916176-03-7

　　　　　Library of Congress Cataloging
Wickstrom, Lois, 1948-
　Oliver / written by Lois Wickstrom ; illustrated by Priscilla Marden.
　p. cm.
Summary: Oliver, a lizardlike animal who has been adopted, sulks after being scolded and wonders what his "real" parents are like.
　ISBN 0-9611872-5-5 : $14.95
　1. Adoption—Fiction. 2. Parent and child—Fiction. 3. Animals—Fiction I. Marden, Priscilla, ill. II. Title. PZ7.W629401 1991
—dc20　　　　　　　　　90-40133
　　　　　　　　　CIP
　　　　　　　　　AC

Oliver lives with a mommy and a daddy and a goldfish. He is related to his mom and dad by love and law. Oliver was adopted.

One day when Oliver was playing pirate on the sidewalk, he decided to climb the new maple tree, the mast of his pirate ship. From there he could see if any treasure ships were near.

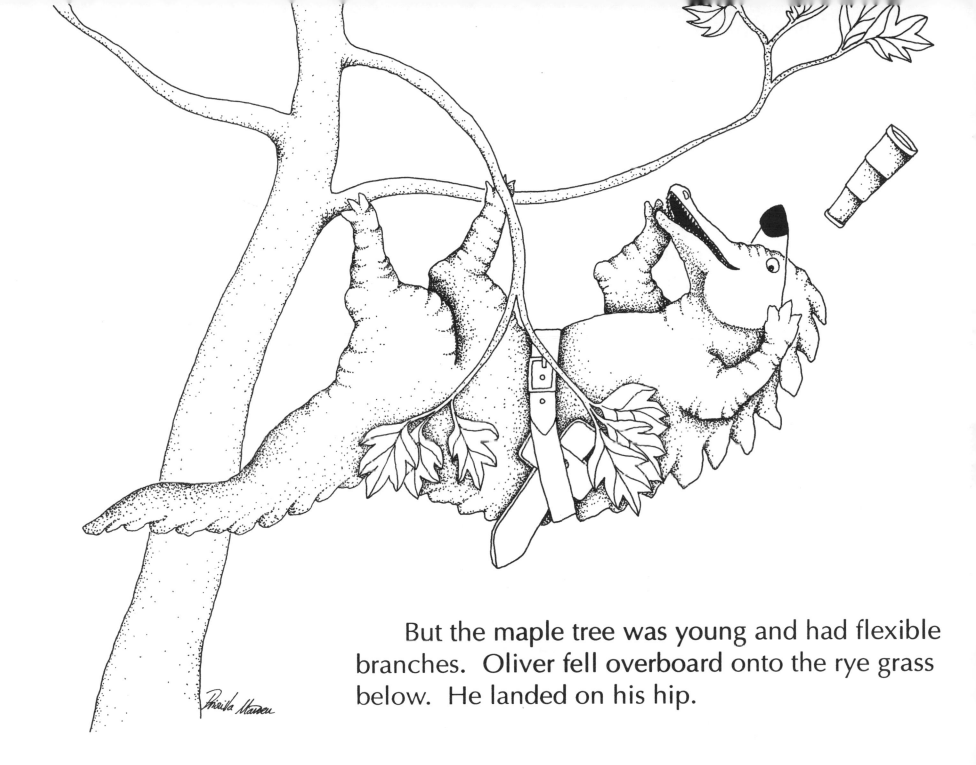

But the **maple tree was young** and had flexible branches. Oliver fell overboard onto the rye grass below. He landed on his hip.

His daddy rushed over to see if he had broken any bones.

"Are you all right? Where do you hurt?" he asked.

"I'm just bumped," said Oliver, pointing to his hip.

His daddy kissed him and then he said, "It's not a good idea to climb a tree that isn't strong. Now go upstairs to your room and think about how to play safely."

On his way upstairs, Oliver thought, "Daddy doesn't understand that the maple tree looks more like a ship's mast than any other tree on the block."

In his room, Oliver started to cry and feel sorry for himself. He beat up his pillow so hard that he ripped the pillowcase. He felt so angry that he was sure he'd poke himself if he tried to sew it up.

"I wouldn't be stuck in this room if I hadn't been adopted," he moped.

Oliver tried to imagine what his birthparents were doing, and what he might be doing, himself, if he were with them instead of being stuck in his room.

Maybe his birthparents worked for the fire department.
Then he could ride the fire truck everywhere they went.

Maybe they worked in a skyscraper office building downtown.
Then he could ride the elevator all the way up and down.

Maybe his birthparents were scientists.
Then he could do magic with a flip of his wrists.

Maybe his birthparents were so young that they still went to school. Then he could teach them about the multiplication rule.

Maybe he had no birthparents to be found.
They might be dead and buried in the ground.

Maybe they were old and not working anymore.
They might tell him tales from many a distant shore.

Maybe they spoke French or Spanish and lived in another place.
Maybe they were astronauts who flew in outer space.

Maybe he would have lived with only a mommy or a daddy. Or he might have been part of a great big family.

But then Oliver sadly recalled that his birthparents weren't ready to be parents when he was born. He didn't know why. But he did know that it wasn't because they didn't want to be his parents. They just couldn't be parents to any baby right then.

So whatever they were doing, he couldn't be with them. And he was stuck in his room with a torn pillowcase that he really ought to be mending.

So Oliver decided to sneak downstairs to get the sewing box from the dining room table. As he got near, he heard his mommy calling from the kitchen.

Oliver went to his mother.

"We've been baking cookies. Would you like to lick the bowl?" she asked.

"Yum! Yes, please!" shouted Oliver as he grabbed the bowl off the counter.

Oliver shared the bowl with his mommy, and his daddy licked the beater.

When they were done, Oliver said, "I was thinking about being adopted. I could be having a whole different life."

"That's true," agreed Daddy. "I used to think that I was adopted and my parents just hadn't told me about it. I was sure that I really belonged to a circus family that would let me stay up late and go barefoot."

"I thought I was adopted, too," said Mommy. "And that my birth family had lots of horses and I would get to ride them."

"But you two weren't adopted, were you?" asked Oliver.

"No," said Mommy.

"No," said Daddy. "But I think most children imagine other lives they could be having, especially when they are angry with their parents."

"Then I guess I'll stay with you two," said Oliver. "But first I'll have to mend my pillowcase."

And since he wasn't angry anymore, he didn't poke himself.

Author Information

Lois Wickstrom has written other books, including <u>Ladybugs</u> <u>for</u> <u>Loretta</u>, and <u>Food</u> <u>Conspiracy</u> <u>Cookbook</u>. She is also the creator of the "It's Chemical" video series which teaches chemical concepts in a situation comedy format for upper elementary and junior high students.

Artist Information

Priscilla Marden is a graphic designer specializing in wildlife illustration and New Age marketing. She lives in a log cabin in the wilds of Moose, Wyoming, with her two sons and an assortment of wild and domestic critters.

Other OUR CHILD PRESS Titles

Is That Your Sister? by Catherine and Sherry Bunin

Kids are always asking Catherine, "Is that your sister?" Catherine and Carla are sisters but they don't look at all alike. This is easy for Catherine to explain: "I tell the kids my sister and I were adopted." Then they ask her, "What's adopted?" A true story of how one family grew by adoption.

Don't Call Me Marda by Sheila Kelly Welch

Adopt a retarded kid! Why would anyone want to do that -- especially your own parents? Told from the perspective of an eleven-year-old, this illustrated novel explains in detail the joys, frustrations, challenges and triumphs of opening your hearts and homes to waiting children. A perfect gift to share with friends and family.

Our Child: Preparation for Parenting in Adoption -- Instructor's Guide by Carol Hallenbeck

A detailed curriculum guide to be used by those who believe in preparation for parenthood education. Designed specifically to meet the needs of couples who build their families by adoption.

Supporting an Adoption by Pat Holmes

Friends and family are often not enthusiastic about an adoption and usually don't know what to say or do. Help them! This little booklet tells them what helps and what hurts. Give your family and friends a copy today!

OUR CHILD PRESS
800 MAPLE GLEN LANE
WAYNE PA 19087-4797